Thomas

AND THE PONY SHOW

by Christopher Awdry

illustrated by Ken Stott

Heinemann • London

First published in Great Britain 1993
by William Heinemann Ltd, an imprint of
Reed Children's Books Limited,
Michelin House, 81 Fulham Road, London SW3 6RB
AUCKLAND · MELBOURNE · SINGAPORE · TORONTO
Copyright © William Heinemann Ltd 1993

Printed in Great Britain

Thomas was waiting at the station for the guard to blow his whistle and wave his flag. He saw Becky and her mother come onto the platform.

Thomas knew Becky well. He often saw her riding her pony, Barnaby, as he puffed past the farm where she lived.

Sometimes she would be jumping Barnaby. Thomas was careful not to whistle in case he frightened the pony.

There was to be a Pony Show in Fox's Field. Thomas watched the men preparing for it as he passed.

" I wish I could see the Pony Show," he thought.
" Becky is sure to be there riding Barnaby."

The day of the show was beautiful and sunny.
Thomas hummed happily as he ran along the rails.

But as he came round a curve in the line, he saw
a horsebox standing on the road.

Becky stood beside the horsebox looking worried.
Her father was bending down beside the front
wheels.

" It looks as if they have broken down," said Thomas's driver. "Poor Becky. She will be disappointed if she has to miss the show."

When Thomas reached the next station, he saw the
Stationmaster talking to the Fat Controller.
A porter was waiting nearby.

While Thomas stood in the station, the porter
spoke to the guard. Then Percy arrived, pushing
a horsebox. Carefully they coupled it to Clarabel.

The guard went to tell Thomas's driver: "Becky was on her way to the Pony Show with Barnaby when her horsebox broke down.

The Fat Controller has asked if Thomas will take
Barnaby, Becky and her mother on to the Show.
Her father will wait for the breakdown lorry."

The ticket collector shook his head as the
pony was led onto the platform. "Most unusual," he said,
as the porter opened the doors of the horsebox.

Becky and her mother walked Barnaby up the ramp
and when the pony was safely shut in the stall, they
sat down at the back and Thomas set off again.

Fox's Field was near the next station. Quickly
Becky led Barnaby out of the horsebox and
trotted him to the starting point.

Thomas was glad to see she was smiling again.
As she reached the starting point her name was
called out. She was only just in time.

While Thomas watched, Barnaby jumped a clear round.
Everyone clapped and Thomas whistled excitedly:
" Peep pip pip peeeeeeep."

But Thomas had to go before the results were announced. "I wonder if Becky will get a prize?" he kept saying. "I do hope so."

The next day, Becky and Barnaby were waiting for him at the station. Barnaby was wearing a big red rosette, and Becky had brought a yellow one for Thomas.

" Thank you, Thomas," she said happily. "We would
never have won without you."
Thomas was happy too.